Abigail's Auntie Kristi

Allison Romero

Illustrations by Uğur Köse

A Grackle Book

Grackle Publishing - Ambler, Pennsylvania

Grackle
An imprint of Grackle Publishing, LLC
gracklepublishing.com

In loving memory of

Auntie Kristi

Abigail watched the clock, trying her very best to be patient.

Whenever Abigail was really excited about something, each minute seemed to go by so slowly.

Today would be a super fun day, so time seemed super slow.

Today was Abigail's spa day with Auntie Kristi. That meant a Frappuccino, a pedicure, and maybe even a special lunch.

The doorbell!

Abigail ran to answer the door as Mommy followed.

"Corn Cob!" Auntie Kristi exclaimed, reaching out for a hug. Abigail happily wrapped her arms around Auntie Kristi and felt her warm hug.

"Hi, Ally Bear!" Mommy smiled and hugged Auntie Kristi as Abigail laughed at Auntie Kristi's silly nickname for Mommy.

"Thank you for doing this. Abigail has been looking forward to her pedicure all week."

"Of course! My toes need some love. Are you ready to go, Corn Cob?"

"Yes!" Abigail hugged Mommy goodbye, then grabbed Auntie Kristi's hand and off they went.

After a short drive and a quick stop at Starbucks, Abigail and Auntie Kristi settled into their comfy chairs at the spa.

Abigail glanced at the bottles of nail polish. She instantly knew which color she would pick for herself.

Auntie Kristi held up two bottles. "Which one do you like for me, the pink or the blue?"

Abigail examined the two polishes closely, taking her aunt's question very seriously.

"Hmm, I like the pink."

Auntie Kristi looked at the colors carefully, then nodded. "I agree." She set the blue aside and held on to the pink.

Auntie Kristi sipped her chai tea while Abigail drank her vanilla bean Frappuccino.

"Auntie Kristi?"

"Yes?"

"I love our spa days."

"Aw, Baby Shark, I love them too." Abigail smiled at Auntie Kristi's second favorite nickname for her. To Auntie Kristi, she was never just Abigail.

The lady covered Abigail's toenails in a pretty yellow.

"Ooh, I like that color, Corn Cob. Good choice!"

Abigail giggled. "Auntie Kristi, why do you call me Corn Cob?"

"Because the first time I felt you kick in your mommy's tummy, your mommy said that you were the size of a corn cob. So, you are my little Corn Cob."

Abigail smiled. "If I'm your Corn Cob, then what are you?"

"I'm your Auntie Kristi, silly Corn Cob! I will always be your Auntie Kristi."

The women finished painting Abigail's and Auntie Kristi's nails then gave them a nice foot massage.

"OK, off to lunch!"

Abigail finished tying her shoes and followed Auntie Kristi out the door.

"Where are we going this time, Auntie Kristi?"

"I found a new place I want to try! Do you like spaghetti?"

Abigail's tummy growled as they opened the doors of The Old Spaghetti Factory.

"Wow!" Abigail had never seen anything like it—a real train car inside the restaurant!

Auntie Kristi looked at the train car with Abigail and smiled. She turned to the man showing them to their table and pointed. "May we have a table inside the car, please?"

The man peeked into the car and nodded. "It's your lucky day! There's a table available."

Abigail felt like the most special girl in the restaurant as she slid into the little booth by the train window. How did Auntie Kristi always make her days so special?

By the time they were done eating, Abigail was tired and ready to go home.

Auntie Kristi walked Abigail to the door and gave her a big hug.

"I will always love you, my little Corn Cob."

Abigail hugged her back. "I love you too, Auntie Kristi."

A Grackle Book

CPSIA information can be obtained
at www.ICGtesting.com
Printed in the USA
BVHW091247050821
613738BV00011B/151